To Terry, Barry, Lenny,
Mary and Sambo

LADYBIRD BOOKS, INC.
Auburn, Maine 04210 U.S.A.
© LADYBIRD BOOKS LTD 1992
Loughborough, Leicestershire, England

Printed in U.S.A.

The Airplane Ride

By Lucinda McQueen and Jeremy Guitar

Ladybird Books

Five little kitten brothers and sisters jostled and clattered about the kitchen.

"Why don't you go out and play?" said Mother Cat, who wanted a chance to do her chores in peace. She held the door open, and the five little kittens scurried outside.

"Stay out of mischief and maybe you'll have a nice surprise later," Mother Cat called after them.

The kittens gathered around their old seesaw in the back yard.

"What'll we do?" asked Trudy, the littlest.

"We could go down to the river," said her brother Lenny.

"Naw," said Nat, the oldest, peering over the hedgerow at their mother in the kitchen. "We have to stay out of trouble."

Just then Nat spied a poster on the building next door. It read, "COME TO THE CIRCUS! SEE ELEPHANTS AND ACROBATS AND A DAREDEVIL AIRPLANE PILOT!"

"I've got it!" exclaimed Nat. "Let's make a pretend airplane out of the seesaw!"

"That's a great idea!" chorused Alice and Willy, the twins. "We can use the garbage can for the front."

"And the shovel for the tail," said Lenny.

"How about the lawn mower for the wheels?" said little Trudy.

Whooping and shouting, they all rushed off to gather their pieces.

Mother Cat saw a flurry of activity as she looked out the kitchen window. The kittens were scuttling back and forth across the yard. Each time they passed the window, she saw them disappear behind the hedgerow with some implement or other.

Even little Trudy was working hard, trundling across the grass with the lawn mower.

"What good children they are!" thought Mother Cat. "They must be tidying up the yard."

Meanwhile, behind the hedgerow, the airplane was taking shape. The seesaw was teetering on lawn mower wheels, with the wheelbarrow balanced on one end. The garbage can was stuck on top of the wheelbarrow. A ladder was tied crosswise with ropes and covered with bed sheets.

"Okay!" shouted Nat at last. "We're finished. Let's give her a push up the hill, and then we'll coast down."

The kittens shoved their pretend airplane with all their might. As they reached the top of the hill, the airplane gave a lurch, then began rolling down. Faster and faster it went, as they all piled onto it.

"Hang on, we're going over a bump!" cried Lenny from the front.

The passengers all shut their eyes as the speeding junk pile vaulted into the air. They braced themselves for the crash.

But it never came. One by one the kittens opened their eyes.
The neighborhood was rushing by below them!

"We're flying!" they screeched in amazement. "We're
really flying!"

The seesaw fluttered crazily through the sky, then began to spiral about. Suddenly the kittens' own back yard rushed up to meet them. As the wheelbarrow wheel skidded over the tops of the bushes, the whole contraption flew apart in all directions.

The kittens rolled head over heels across the yard. They ended up in a pile of leaves at one end of the garden.

Cautiously they crept up to the hedgerow and peeked in the kitchen window. Their mother was hanging up her dishcloth.

Just then Mother Cat looked up and noticed the kittens. "You've been so well behaved!" she called out the window. "Come in and get ready for your surprise!"

The five trudged toward the house, brushing bits of grass and leaves from their fur.

"Guess what!" said Mother Cat. "I'm taking you to the circus this afternoon. They have a daredevil pilot in a real airplane, and you can all have rides!"

The five little kittens quietly
followed their mother out the door and headed for the circus.